THE RED BOOK

OR

HOW TO PLAY INDIAN

DIRECTIONS FOR ORGANIZING
A TRIBE OF BOY INDIANS,
MAKING THEIR TEPEES ETC.
IN TRUE INDIAN STYLE

—

BY
ERNEST THOMPSON SETON

British Library Cataloguing-in-Publication Data
A catalogue record for this book is available from the
British Library

Ernest Thompson Seton

Ernest Thompson Seton was born on 14th August 1860, in South Shields, County Durham, England. He grew up to be a pioneering author, wildlife artist, founder of the Woodcraft Indians, and one of the originators of the Boy Scouts of America (BSA).

The Seton family emigrated to Canada when Ernest was just six years old, and most of his childhood was consequently spent in Toronto. As a youth, he retreated to the woods to draw and study animals as a way of avoiding his abusive father – a practice which shaped the rest of his adult life. On his twenty-first birthday, Seton's father presented him with a bill for all the expenses connected with his childhood and youth, including the fee charged by the doctor who delivered him. He paid the bill, but never spoke to his father again.

Originally known as Ernest Evan Thompson, Ernest changed his name to Ernest Thompson Seton, believing that Seton had been an important name in his paternal line. He became successful as a writer, artist and naturalist, and moved to New York City to further his career. Seton later lived at 'Wyndygoul', an estate that he built in Cos Cob, a section of Greenwich, Connecticut. After experiencing vandalism by some local youths, Seton invited the young miscreants to his estate for a weekend, where he told them what he claimed were stories of the American Indians and of nature.

After this experience, he formed the Woodcraft Indians (an American youth programme) in 1902 and invited the local youth to join (at first just boys, but later girls as well). The stories that Seton told became a series of articles written for the *Ladies Home Journal*, and were eventually collected in *The Birch Bark Roll of the Woodcraft Indians* in 1906. Seton also met Scouting's founder, Lord Baden-Powell, in 1906. Baden-Powell had read Seton's book of stories, and was greatly intrigued by it. After the pair had met and shared ideas, Baden-Powell went on to found the Scouting movement worldwide, and Seton became vital in the foundation of the Boy Scouts of America (BSA) and was its first Chief Scout (from 1910 – 1915). Despite this large achievement, Seton quickly became embroiled in disputes with the BSA's other founders, Daniel Carter Beard and James E. West.

In addition to disputes about the content of Seton's contributions to the Boy Scout Handbook, conflicts also arose about the suffrage activities of his wife, Grace, and his British citizenship (it being *an American* organization). In his personal life, Seton was married twice. The first time was to Grace Gallatin in 1896, with whom he had one daughter, Ann (who later changed her name to Anya), and secondly to Julia M. Buttree, with whom he adopted an infant daughter, Beulah (who also changed her first name, to Dee). Alongside his work with the Woodcraft Indians and the BSA, Seton also found time to pursue his primary interest – that of nature writing.

Seton was an early pioneer of animal fiction writing, his most popular work being *Wild Animals I Have Known* (1898), which contains the story of his killing of the wolf Lobo. He later became involved in a literary debate known as the nature fakers controversy, after John Burroughs published an article in 1903 in the *Atlantic Monthly* attacking writers of sentimental animal stories. The controversy lasted for four years and included important

American environmental and political figures of the day, including President Theodore Roosevelt. Seton was also associated with the Santa Fe arts and literary community during the mid-1930s and early 1940s, which comprised a group of artists and authors including author and artist Alfred Morang, sculptor and potter Clem Hull, painter Georgia O'Keeffe, painter Randall Davey, painter Raymond Jonson, leader of the Transcendental Painters Group, and artist Eliseo Rodriguez.

In 1931, Seton became a United States citizen. He died on 23rd October, 1946 (aged eighty-six) in Seton Village in northern New Mexico. Seton was cremated in Albuquerque. In 1960, in honour of his 100th birthday and the 350th anniversary of Santa Fe, his daughter Dee and his grandson, Seton Cottier (son of Anya), in a fitting tribute to the man who loved his surrounding countryside so much, scattered his ashes over Seton Village from an airplane.

TO ORGANIZE A BAND
OF INDIANS

HE Woodcraft Indians have been organized to give young people the advantages of camp life without its dangers.

The Indian plan has been adopted in preference to others because its picturesqueness takes immediate and complete hold of the boys.

Most boys love to play Indian and would like to learn more about doing it. They want to know about all the interesting Indian things that are possible for them to do. It adds a great pleasure to the lives of such boys when they know that they can go out in the holidays and camp in the woods just as the Indians did, and make all their own weapons in Indian style as well as rule themselves after the manner of a band of Redmen.

Of course there are many bad Indians, and many bad things are done by nearly all Indians, but we wish to imitate the good things of good Indians. Our watchword then is: "The best things of the best Indians," and our object: "The study and pleasures of Woodcraft."

Our tribes are trained in Woodcraft and in Self-government. By Woodcraft we mean out-door athletics, nature study and camping as a fine art.

Photography is recognized as a branch of nature study, and camper-craft is made to include the simplest methods of triangulation, starcraft, finding one's way, telling direction, sign-language, as well as many branches of Indian craft.

About one hundred deeds or exploits are recognized in these departments and the braves are given decorations that show what they have achieved.

The plan aims to give the young people "something to do, something to think about and something to enjoy in the woods," with a view always to character building.

First: Get the boys (or girls) together, any number from three upwards, and by popular vote elect the following officers:

Head War Chief elected by the Tribe. He should be strong as well as popular, because his duties are to lead and to enforce the laws. He is head of the Council.

Second War Chief, to take the Head Chief's place when he is absent, otherwise he is merely a Councillor.

Third War Chief, for leader when the other two are away.

Wampum Chief. He has charge of the money and public property of the Tribe, except the records. He obeys the Head Chief and Council. He ought to have a lock box or small trunk to keep valuables in. Squaws are eligible.

Chief of the Painted Robe, or Feather-tally. He keeps the tribal records, including the Redbook, the Roster or Roll, the Winter Count, or Record of Camps and Seasons, and the Feather-tally or record of honors and exploits. He enters nothing except on instructions from the Council. He should be an artist. Squaws are eligible.

Chief of the Council-Fire. It is his exclusive privilege to make fire. He must do it without matches. He must also see that the camp and woods are kept clean. Squaws are eligible.

Sometimes one Brave or Chief holds more than one of these last three offices.

The Head Chief may add a *Chief Medicine Man* or *Woman* to the Council without regard to age, attainments or position. (In one case the Head Chief made his own mother Medicine Woman.) And the tribe may vote in a second medicine man. Their duty is to advise the Head Chief.

Add to these not more than twelve elected Councillors and all the Sachems (see p. 24).

All are under the Chief. All disputes, etc., are settled by the Chief and Council. The Council makes the laws and fixes the dues. The Chief enforces the laws.

All officers are elected for one year or until their successors are chosen. The election to take place as soon as possible after Spring Day, the first of March.

(Whenever in doubt we try to follow the U. S. Constitution.)

VOW OF THE HEAD CHIEF
(To be signed with his name and totem in the tally-book.)

I solemnly promise to maintain the laws and to see fair play in all the doings of the Tribe.

VOW OF EACH BRAVE ON JOINING
(To be signed with the name and totem of each in the tally-book.)

I solemnly promise that I will obey the Chief and Council of my Tribe, and if I fail in my duty I will appear before the Council and submit without murmuring to their decision.

LAWS

1. Don't rebel. *Rebellion* by any one against any decision of the Council is punishable by expulsion. Absolute obedience is always enforced.

2. Don't kindle a wild fire. To start a wild fire— that is, to set the woods or prairies afire—is a crime against the State, as well as the Tribe. Never leave a fire in camp without some one to watch it

3. Don't harm song-birds. It is forbidden to kill or injure or frighten song-birds, or to disturb their nests or eggs, or to molest squirrels.

4. Don't break the Game Laws.

5. Don't cheat. Cheating in the games or records or wearing honors not conferred by the Council is a crime.

6. Don't bring firearms of any kind into camp. Bows and arrows are enough for our purpose.

7. Don't make a dirty camp. Keep the woods clean by burying all garbage.

8. No smoking (for those under 18).

9. No fire-water in camp.

Punishments are meted out by the Chief and Council after a hearing of the case. They consist of:

Exclusion from the games for a time.

Of tasks of drudgery and camp service.

Of reduction in rank.

The extreme penalty is banishment from the Tribe.

TOTEM

The totem of the whole nation of Seton Indians (as they have called themselves) is the White or Silver Buffalo.

Each Band needs a totem of its own in addition. This is selected by the Council, and should be something easy to draw. Each brave adds a private totem of his own, usually a drawing of his name.

The first of these Indians took as their totem a Blue Buffalo and so became Blue Buffalo Band, and

Deerfoot, the Chief, uses the Blue Buffalo totem with his own added underneath.

Any bird, animal, tree or flower will do. It is better if it have some special reason.

One Tribe set out on a long journey to look for a totem. They agreed to take the first living wild thing that they saw and knew the name of. They traveled all one day and saw nothing to suit, but next day in a swamp they startled a Blue Heron. It went off with a harsh cry. So they became the "Blue Herons," and adopted as a warcry the croak of the bird—"Hrrrrr—Blue Heron." Another Band have the Wolf totem. Another the Flying Eagle, and yet another the Snapping-turtle.

DECORATIONS

The most important is, of course, the War Bonnet of Eagle feathers. This is a full record of the owner's exploits, as well as a grand decoration. It is fully described in "The Ladies' Home Journal" for July, 1902.

The feathers are made of white goose quill feathers, the tip dyed black, a leather loop is lashed to the quill end of each to fasten it onto the hat band. Each feather stands for an exploit and is awarded by the Council. If it was Grand Coup or High Honor the feather had a tuft of red horsehair lashed on the top.

The feathers are held in place by a lace through the bottom loop to hold them to the body of the cap, and a stout thread through the middle of each midrib, stringing them together and holding them the right distance apart.

One cannot always wear the war bonnet, yet most want to wear a visible record of their rank. To meet this need we have a badge adapted from an old Iroquois silver brooch.

In this the White or Silver Buffalo represents the whole nation. The owner can put his initials on the Buffalo's forehead, if desired.

The pin in the middle is in the real Indian style. To fasten the brooch on you throw back the pin, then work a pucker of the coat through the opening from behind. When it sticks out far enough bend it to one side, pierce it with the pin, then put the pin down and work the pucker back smooth. This can never work loose or get lost.

The rank of the wearer is thus shown:

The ordinary brave or squaw as soon as admitted wears the simple badge, so—

Ordinary Brave or Squaw.

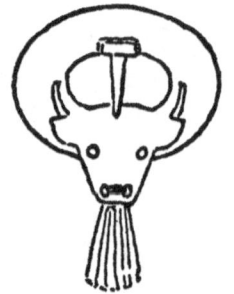

Councillor.

Every one in the Council is a Councillor Chief, and adds a beard to the Buffalo, using silk, wool or thread through the nostrils.

The Medicine Man adds a criss-cross from left eye to right nostril, and right eye to left nostril. Of course if he is on the Council he also adds the beard.

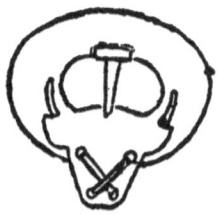

Medicine Man

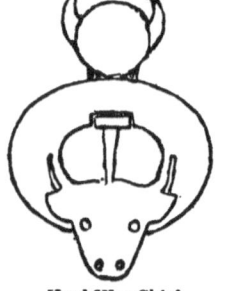

Head War Chief.

The Head Chief wears, in addition to the beard, a horned shield. On the circle of the shield is engraved the totem of the Tribe.

The horns are worn only by a Head Chief. The following shows their importance:

"No one wears the headdress surmounted with horns except the dignitaries who are very high in authority and whose exceeding valor, worth and power are admitted by all the nation.

"This man (Mah-to-toh-pa) was the only man in the nation who was allowed to wear the horns, and all, I found, looked upon him as the leader who had the power to lead all the warriors in time of war." (Catlin, Vol. 1, p. 103.)

The second warchief wears the same badge as the first except that it has but one horn (the right) on the shield.

The third warchief wears the same with left horn only on shield.

Scalps. Each warrior wears a long tuft of horsehair. This answers as his scalp. He can lose this only in an important competition, approved by the Council, in which he stakes his scalp against that of some other Brave. If he loses he surrenders his tuft to the winner and goes tuftless until the Council think proper to give him a new scalp.

But the winner keeps the old scalp for a teepee or other decoration, and counts Coup or Grand Coup, as the Council may decide. The warrior without tuft cannot sit in Council or take part in the competitions.

TEEPEES

MANY famous campers have said that the Indian teepee is the best known movable home. It is roomy, self-ventilating, can scarcely blow down, and is the only tent that admits of fire inside.

Then why is it not everywhere used? Because of the difficulty of the poles. If on the prairie you must carry your poles. If in the woods you must cut them at each camp.

General Sibley, the famous Indian fighter, invented a teepee with a single pole, and this is still used by our army. But it will not do for us. Its one pole is made in part of iron and is very cumbersome, as well as costly. The "Sibley" is ugly, too, compared with a real teepee, and we are "Playing Injun," not soldier, so we shall stick to the famous and picturesque old teepee of the real Buffalo Indians.

In the "Buffalo days" this teepee was made of Buffalo skin; now it is made of some sort of canvas or cotton, but it is decorated much in the old style. I tried to get an extra fine one made by the Indians especially as a model for our boys, but I found that no easy matter. I could not go among the Red-folk and order it as in a department store.

The making of a teepee was serious business, to be approached in a serious manner. Only an experienced old squaw could do it, and she must dream and think, for perhaps weeks, first; then having worked out a plan in her mind she must call in a dozen of her neighbors to make a "bee" and carry out her exact plan. Any change is "bad medicine" —that is, "unlucky." I waited a year and the tent-making spirit kept away; none of the squaws felt moved to build a teepee, and I was in a quandary.

One of the Chiefs suggested that if I waited another year I might get one. When the Buffalo came back I should be sure of it.

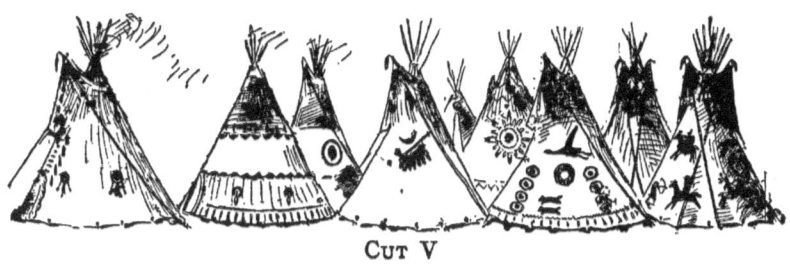

CUT V

At length I solved the difficulty by buying one ready made from Thunder Bull, a Chief of the Cheyennes.

It appears at the left end of the row in the above cut. This is an 18-foot teepee and is large enough for twenty boys to live in. A large one is easier to keep clear of smoke, but most boys will prefer a smaller one, as it is much handier, cheaper and easier to make. I shall therefore give the working plan of a 10-foot teepee of the simplest form—the raw material of which can be bought new for less than $4.00. This is big enough for four, or perhaps five, boys.

It requires 22 square yards of 6 or 8-ounce duck, heavy unbleached muslin or Canton flannel (the wider the better, as that saves labor in making up), which costs about $3.00; 75 feet of 3-16-inch clothesline, 15 cents; string for sewing rope ends, etc., 5 cents.

Of course one can often pick up second-hand materials that are quite good and cost next to nothing. An old wagon cover, or two or three old sheets, will make the teepee, and even if they are patched it is all right, the Indian teepees are often mended where bullets and arrows went through them. Scraps of rope, if not rotted, will work in well enough.

Supposing you have new material to deal with. Get it machine-run together, 20 feet long and 10 feet wide. Lay this down perfectly flat (Cut VI). On a peg or nail at A in the middle of the long side put a 10-foot cord loosely, and then with a burnt stick in a loop at the other end draw the half-circle B C D. Now cut out the two little triangles at A each 6 inches on each side. Cut the canvas along these dotted lines. From the scraps left over cut two pieces for smoke-flaps, as shown.

the long corner of each (H in No. 1, I in. No. 2) a small three-cornered piece is sewed, to make a pocket for the end of the pole.

Now sew the smoke-flaps to the cover so that M L of No. 1 is fitted to P E, and N O of No. 2 to Q G.

Two inches from the edge B P make a double row of holes; each hole is 2 inches from its mate, and each pair is 5 inches from the next pair, except at the 2-foot space marked "door," where no holes are needed.

The holes on the other side, Q D, must exactly fit on these.

At A fasten a strong 4 -foot cord by the middle. Fasten the end of a 10-foot cord to J and

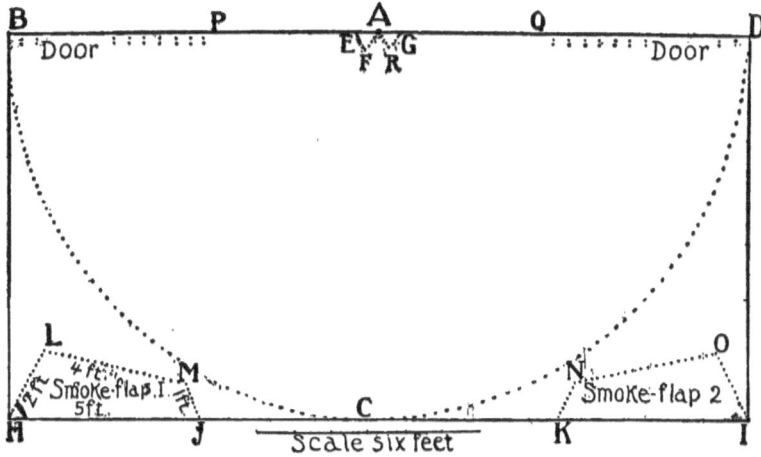

CUT VI—Pattern of 10-Foot Tepee.

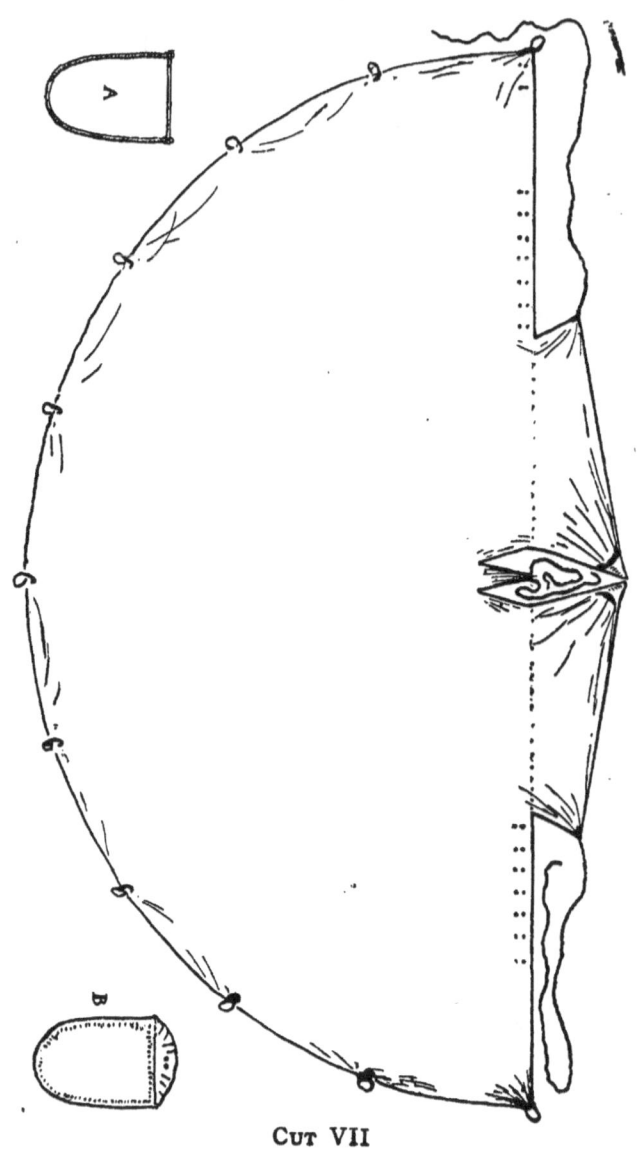

CUT VII

another to K. Hem a rope all along on the bottom B C D. Cut 12 pieces of rope each about 15 inches long, fasten one very firmly to the canvas at B, another at the point D, and the rest at regular distances to the hem-rope along the edge between, for peg-loops. The tepee cover is now made. (See Cut VII.)

For the door (some never use one) take a limber sapling ¾-inch thick and 5 1-2 feet long, also one 22 inches long. Bend the long one into a horseshoe and fasten the short one across the ends (A in Cut VII). On this stretch canvas, leaving a flap at the top, in the middle of which two small holes are made (B, Cut VII) so as to hang the door on a lacing-pin. Nine of these lacing-pins are needed. They are of smooth, round, straight hardwood, a foot long and 1-4-inch thick. The way of skewering the two edges together is seen in the Omaha teepee at the end of the line in Cut IX.

Now all the necessary parts of the teepee cover are made and it appears as in Cut VII. But no real Indian would live in a teepee which was not decorated in some way and it is well to begin the adorning while the cover is flat on the ground. From the centre A at 7 feet distance draw a circle; draw another at 6 1-2 feet, another at 3 feet and another at 2 1-2 feet (Cut VIII). Make the lines any color you like, put a row of spots or zigzags in each of the 6-inch bands; then on the side, midway between A and C, draw a 1-foot circle.

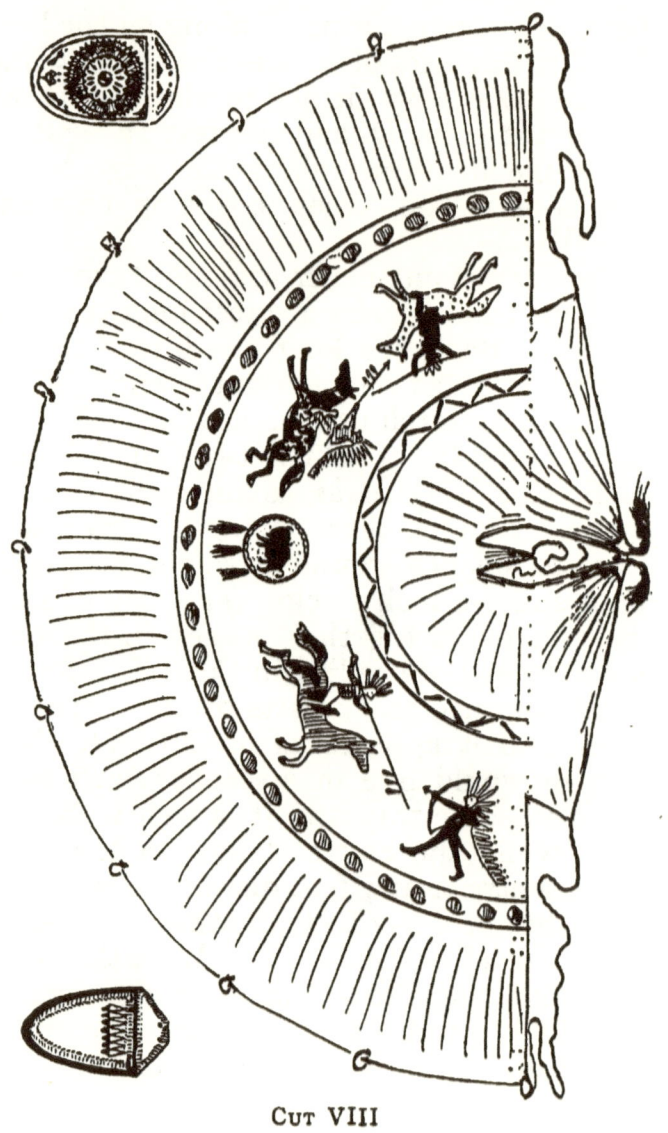

CUT VIII

In the old days every Indian had a "coat-of-arms" or "totem" and this properly appeared on his tent. This little circle is a good place to paint your totem. The spaces at each side can be covered with figures showing the owner's adventures; using flat colors with black outlines, but without shading. Oil colors rubbed on with a stiff brush and little oil are nearest to the old Indian style.

The pictures are usually about the middle of the wall, because when high they get smoked, and when low they get dirty.

In addition to being painted the teepee is usually decorated with Eagle feathers, tufts of horsehair, beadwork, etc. In Cut VIII the owner's crest, a "Blue Buffalo," is shown in the small circle, and from that are three tufts for tails. On the teepees in cuts V and IX are shown many different styles of decoration and all of them were from real teepees. Scalplocks were also used, although horsetails are more often seen now.

Twelve poles also are needed. They should be as straight and smooth as posssible; crooked; rough poles are signs of a bad housekeeper—a squaw is known by her teepee poles. They should be 13 or 14 feet long and about 1 1-2 inches thick or less at the top. Two are for the smoke-vent; they may be more slender than the others. Last of all, make a dozen stout short pegs about 15 inches long and about 1 1-2 inches thick.

Drive a small stake in the ground where the center of the teepee will come and about this as a center mark a circle the same diameter as the tent. For a ten foot teepee a ten foot circle, etc.

This is how the teepee is put up:—

With one end of a twenty foot rope tie together three of the poles at a point as high as the width of the canvas. Set them as a tripod, their ends touching the edge of the circle. Then set up the other poles (except three, including the two slender ones,) for the frame of the teepee, their ends on the circumference of the circle, their tops resting in the angles of the tripod. Now with the loose end of the twenty foot rope bind all the poles where they cross by walking several times around the frame, on the outside, and drawing the rope tight as you go. The loose end may then be left hanging down inside for an anchor.

Now fasten the rope at A to the stout pole left over at a point 10 feet up. Raise this into its place and the teepee cover with it, opposite where the door is to be. Carry the two wings of the tent around till they overlap and fasten together with the lacing-pins. Put the end of a vent-pole in each of the vent-flap pockets, outside of the teepee. Peg down the edges of the canvas at each loop if a storm is coming, otherwise a few will do. Hang the door on a convenient lacing-pin. Drive a stout stake inside the teepee, tie the anchor rope to this and the teepee is ready for weather. In the center dig a hole 18 inches wide and 6 inches deep for the fire. The fire is the great advantage of the teepee, and the smoke the great disadvantage, but experience will show how to manage this. Keep the smoke-vent swung down wind, or at least quartering down. Sometimes you must leave the door a little open or raise the bottom of the teepee cover a little on the windward side. If this makes too much draft on your back stretch a piece of canvas between two or three of the poles inside the teepee, in front of the opening made and reaching to the ground. This is a lining or dew-cloth. The draft will go up behind this.

By these tricks you can make the vent draw the smoke. But, after all, the main thing is to use only the best and dryest of wood. This makes a clear fire. There will always be more or less smoke 7 or 8 feet up, but it worries no one there and it keeps the mosquitoes away. When these pests were very bad I used sometimes to "smudge" my teepee—that is, throw an armful of green leaves or grass on the fire and then run out, close the door and smoke-vent tight, and wait an hour before reentering. The dense smoke would kill or drive out all the mosquitoes in the tent, and the rest of the night there was enough of it hanging around the vent to keep the little plagues away till morning.

You should always be ready for a storm over night. Keep a stock of dry firewood in the teepee. You must study the wind continually and be weatherwise—that is, a woodcrafter—if you are to make a success of the teepee.

And remember this: The Indians did not look for hardships. They took care of their health so as to withstand hardship when it came, but they made themselves as comfortable as possible. They never slept on the ground if they could help it. Catlin tells us of the beautiful 4-post beds the Mandans used to make in their lodges. The Blackfeet make neat beds of willow rods carefully peeled, and the Eastern Indians cut piles of pine and fir branches to keep them off the ground. Failing these they used hay or straw. The bed material should be kept together by small logs put at each side.

During long heavy rains some of the Indians used to put a "bull-boat" over the smoke-vent of the lodge. We are sometimes forced to do the same. We sew canvas on a frame of willow hoops which is about 3 feet across and 18 inches deep. This sits on the top of the poles like a cap.

CUT IX

A LIST OF THE EXPLOITS OR COUPS THAT ENTITLE THE BRAVE TO A DECORATION

HESE exploits are intended to distinguish those warriors who are *first class* or *remarkable* in each department. They may be called Honors and High Honors, but the Plains Indians speak of their exploits as *Coup* (pronounced coo) and Grand Coup. The Sioux, I am informed, use the French word *coup*, but call them "*Jus-pee-na Coo*" and "*Tonka Coo*," the "Little Deed" and the "Big Deed."

The decoraton for a Coup of Honor is an eagle feather for the war-bonnet or a wampum medal for the coat, or both.

For the High Honor or Grand Coup the eagle feather has a red tuft of horsehair on the top, and the wampum medal has a red or yellow tassel from its centre.

No one can count both Coup and Grand Coup or repeat their honor in the same department except for Heroism in which each honor is added that previously worn.

No honors are conferred unless the exploit has been properly witnessed or proven, as though for the century bar of the L. A. W.

The exploits in the first group of Class 1, Athletics, are meant for boys under 16, but all the others apply to all ages.

Those with 40 grand coups are Sachems entitled to sit on the Council without election. They are Red Sachems, White Sachems or Blue Sachems, according to the class in which they have won most of their honors.

CLASS I.— RED HONORS

ATHLETICS

(For boys under sixteen)

1. Walk $3\frac{1}{2}$ measured miles in 1 hour (heel and toe) to count coup or honor; or 4 miles to count grand coup or high honor.

2. Walk $\frac{1}{4}$ of a mile in $2\frac{1}{2}$ minutes for coup; in 2 minutes for grand coup.

3. Walk 1 mile in 11 minutes for coup; in 10 minutes for grand coup.

4. Run 100 yards in 12 seconds for coup; in 11 seconds for grand coup.

5. Run 220 yards in 28 seconds for coup; in 26 seconds for grand coup.

6. Run a mile in 5½ minutes for coup; in 5 minutes for grand coup.

7. High standing jump, 3 feet 4 inches for coup; 3 feet 9 inches for grand coup.

8. High running jump, 4 feet 6 inches for coup; 5 feet for grand coup.

9. Standing broad jump, 8 feet for coup; 9 feet for grand coup.

10. Running broad jump, 16 feet for coup; 18 for grand coup.

11. Hammer-throw (12 lbs.), 80 feet for coup; 90 for grand coup.

12. Shot put (12 lbs.), 30 feet for coup; 35 for grand coup.

13. Throwing the regular 4½-oz. baseball 50 yards for coup; 65 for grand coup.

17. One mile on bicycle, 3½ for coup; 3 minutes for grand coup.

18. Skate 100 yards in 12 seconds for coup; 11 seconds for grand coup.

20. Row (single sculls) one mile in 15 minutes for coup; in 12 minutes for grand coup.

21. Paddle (single) one mile in 20 minutes for coup; in 15 minutes for grand coup.

22. Swim 100 yards in any time at all, to count coup; or 200 in 4 minutes, to count grand coup.

23. Go 400 yards in 6 minutes, running 100, rowing 100, walking 100, and swimming 100 (in any order), for coup; do it in 5 minutes, for grand coup.

24. To catch 10 horses in corral, with 10 throws of the lasso, counts coup; to catch 10 on the range in 10 throws, counts a grand coup.

25. To ride a horse one mile in 3 minutes, clearing a 4-foot hurdle, counts coup; to do it in 2 minutes, clearing a 6-foot hurdle, grand coup.

EYESIGHT

31. To spot the Rabbit at 60 yards or to distinguish six Pleiades and see clearly the "Pappoose on the Squaw's back," counts a coup; to spot the Rabbit at 75 yards and see seven Pleiades, counts a far-sight grand coup. (Those who habitually wear glasses may use them in this test.)

32. To make a 75 score in ten tries in the game of *Quicksight* with ten counters, counts coup; a 95 score, counts a grand coup.

HEROISM

33. Honors are allowed for saving human life at risk of one's own; it is a coup or grand coup at the discretion of the Council.

34. If a scalp is won by exceptional prowess the winner counts coup or grand coup, as the Council may decide.

CLASS II.— WHITE HONORS

CAMPER-CRAFT

40. Come to camp through strange woods from a point one mile off in 20 minutes, for coup; in 15, for grand coup.

41. Light 10 camp fires in succession with 10 matches, all at different places, all with stuff found in the woods by the boy himself, one at least to be on a wet day, for coup. If all ten are done on wet days, or if he does 20, of which two are on wet days, it counts grand coup.

42. Light a fire with fire-drill or rubbing sticks, with material of one's own gathering, counts a coup; to do it in one minute, counts a grand coup.

43. To chop down a 6-inch tree in 60 seconds, throwing it to drive a given stake, coup; in 45 seconds, grand coup.

44. Know and name 10 star groups, for coup; know 10 star groups and tell the names and something about at least one star in each, for grand coup.

45. Take the latitude from the stars at night with a cartwheel, or some home-made instrument, within 2 degrees of error, for coup; 1 degree, for grand coup.

46. To guess one inch, one foot, one yard, one rod, one acre, 100 yards, 200 yards, one quarter-mile, one half-mile, and a mile, within 20 per cent.

of average error, for coup; 10 per cent., for grand coup.

47. To measure the height of a tree without climbing, or distance across a river, etc., without crossing, within 10 per cent. of error, for coup; 5 per cent., for grand coup.

48. In sign-talking, to know and use correctly 50 signs, for coup; 100 signs, for grand coup.

50. To make 20 different standard knots in a rope, for coup; 30, for grand coup.

51. To catch a 2-pound trout on a 5-oz. rod with fly, and without assistance, coup; a 3-pound trout, a grand coup.

52. To cast a fly on 5-oz. 9-foot rod, 50 feet for coup; 75 for grand coup.

53. To catch a 5-pound fish on a 5-oz. rod, grand coup.

54, 55, 56, 57. The best dancer, trailer, singer or artist out of 250, counts coup; the best in 500, grand coup.

In these competitive coups the 250 or 500 warriors need not all be present, but they must be represented by their best men.

ARCHERY

61. Make a total score of 300 with 60 shots one or two meets) 4-foot target at 40 yards coup; make 400 for grand coup.

62. Shoot so fast as to have 6 arrows in the air at once, for coup; 7, for grand coup.

63. Send an arrow 150 yards for coup; 200 for grand coup.

64. To hit the Burlap Deer in the heart at 60 yards first shot, counts a coup; at 75 yards, counts a grand coup.

CLASS III.— BLUE HONORS

NATURE STUDY

71. Know and name correctly, *i.e.*, with the accepted English names, according to any standard authority, 25 trees, and tell something interesting about them, counts coup; 50 for grand coup.

72. Know and name correctly 50 of our wild flowers, for coup; 100, for grand coup.

73. Know and name correctly 50 of our native birds as seen mounted in a museum, the female and young to count separately when they are wholly different from the male; this counts coup; 100 birds, for grand coup.

74. Know and name correctly 50 wild birds in the field; this counts coup; 100, grand coup.

75. Recognize 50 wild birds by note, for coup; 100, for grand coup.

76. Know and name correctly 25 wild quadrupeds for coup; know and name correctly 50, and

tell something interesting about each, for grand coup.

77. Know and draw unmistakable pictures of 25 tracks of our four-footed animals, for coup; of 50, for grand coup.

78. Know and name 25 fish, for coup; 50 fish, for grand coup.

79. Know and name 10 different snakes, telling which are poisonous, for coup; 20 snakes, for grand coup.

80. Know and name 50 common toadstools or mushrooms, for coup; 100, for grand coup.

81. Know and name 50 moths, for coup; 100, for grand coup.

82. Know and name 25 butterflies for coup; 50 butterflies, for grand coup.

83. Know and name 50 other insects, for coup; 100, for grand coup.

84. Know and name 7 turtles, for coup; 14, with something interesting, for grand coup.

PHOTOGRAPHY

90. Make a good recognizable photograph of any wild bird larger than a robin, while on its nest, for coup.

91. Make a good photograph of a partridge drumming, for grand coup.

92. Make a good recognizable photograph of a wild animal or fish in the air, for coup, or grand coup, according to merit.

93. Get a good photograph of any wild animal not looking at you, for coup or grand coup, according to merit.

www.ingramcontent.com/pod-product-compliance
Lightning Source LLC
Chambersburg PA
CBHW032123020726
47494CB00007BA/2218